How Do We Use Machines?

Houghton Mifflin Harcourt™

PHOTOGRAPHY CREDITS: COVER ©Andersen Ross/Blend Images/Getty Images; 5 (bl) ©Photodisc/Getty Images; 6 (t) Chris Clinton/Getty Images; 10 (br) ©Alexander Walter/Getty Images; 11 (br) ©VStock/Alamy Images; 11 (bl) ©papa1266/Shutterstock; 13 (b) ©Ted Foxx/Alamy Images; 16 (t) ©Corbis; 17 (tr) © Brand X Pictures/Getty Images; 17 (cr) ©Heath Robbins/Getty Images; 17 (br) ©Ocean/Corbis

Printed in the U.S.A.

ISBN: 978-0-544-07272-5

15 16 17 18 19 20 1083 20 19 18

4500710587 A B C D E F G

Be an Active Reader!

Look for each word in yellow along with its meaning.

force	lever	wedge
gravity	fulcrum	screw
weight	wheel-and-axle	compound machine
work	pulley	
simple machine	inclined plane	

Underlined sentences answer the questions.

How do objects change motion?

How does a force change an object's motion?

How does gravity affect us?

What are simple machines?

How do levers work?

How does a wheel-and-axle work?

How does a pulley work?

What are other simple machines?

How does a screw work?

What happens when we combine simple machines?

How do machines help us do work?

How do objects change motion?

How do objects start moving? Objects start moving when there is a push or a pull. Think about a friend sitting on a swing. You push your friend to make him or her move. Your friend moves away from you when you push him or her. Think about the chair under your desk. You pull the chair out before you sit on it. Each object is now in a different position, or place. How do the swing and the chair move?

Pushes and pulls change the way an object moves.

How does a force change an object's motion?

Suppose you are not able to lift a heavy box. It is filled with books! You give the box a hard push across the floor. You use force to push the box. A **force** is a push or pull. You use a lot of force to push the box or pull a chair if they are heavy. You don't need to use a lot of force to throw a beach ball!

A beach ball is light. It is easy to throw the ball, or push it away from you.

Force can change the motion of an object. When you describe motion, you tell two things. You talk about the object's speed. You also tell about its direction.

Speed is how fast or slow something moves. Direction tells which way an object moves.

Think about playing baseball. The pitcher throws the ball. You hit the ball hard with your bat. The ball moves quickly through the air. Force changed the ball's direction. When you hit the ball, it flew into the air and over the pitcher's head. It went into the stands. You hit a home run!

Force also changed the ball's speed. The pitcher threw the ball fast. But the ball moved faster when your bat hit the ball.

Force stops a ball's motion when you catch it.

How does gravity affect us?

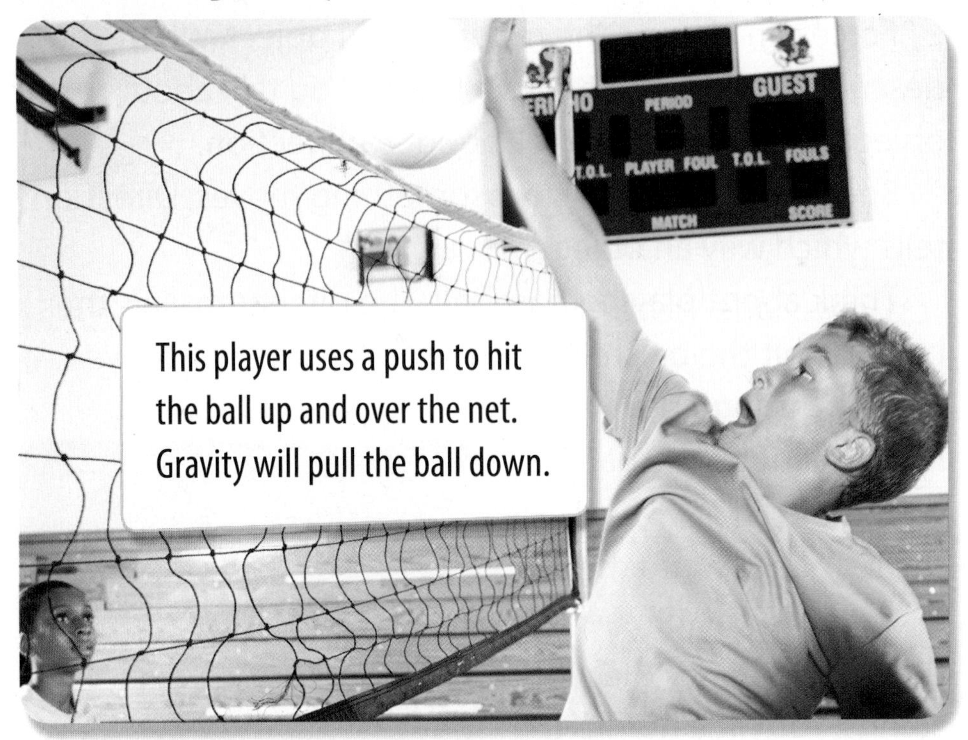

This player uses a push to hit the ball up and over the net. Gravity will pull the ball down.

Do you like playing volleyball? How do you move when you play? You jump up. You hit the ball over the net. What happens when you jump up? Do you fly all the way up into space? No! Something pulls you back down to the ground. It pulls the volleyball down, too. Gravity is a force that pulls objects toward each other. Earth's gravity pulls objects toward its center.

Think about something that you were holding and then dropped. Where did it go? It dropped to the ground! Gravity pulls things toward the ground. Gravity will cause you to fall when you trip.

Gravity affects how much things weigh. Weight is a measure of the force of gravity on an object.

You can use a spring scale to weigh fruit in the grocery store. A heavy fruit will weigh more than a light fruit. An apple will weigh more than a grape.

spring scale

Look at each fruit. Which fruit would weigh the most on the spring scale? Which fruit would weigh the least? Which two fruits would weigh about the same?

What are simple machines?

What does the word *work* mean to you? Is work something you do in school to learn? You may say that the chores you do to help out at home are work.

In science, the word *work* has another meaning. Work is the use of a force—a push or a pull—to move an object. Work moves an object in the same direction as the force. You use simple machines every day to help you work. A simple machine is a tool that makes work easier.

You use force, or a pull, to rake leaves. The rake is a simple machine.

How do levers work?

The tool in the picture is a lever. The painter lowers his hand, and the tool lifts the lid off of the paint can.

Think about lifting a lid off of a paint can. What simple machine can you use to help you?

A lever is a simple machine used to lift things. A lever is a bar that turns on a fixed point. A fixed point does not move. The fixed point on a lever is called the fulcrum. The load is the object you are moving. The load is on one end of the lever. The load moves as you move the other end of the lever.

How does a wheel-and-axle work?

A toy car uses a wheel-and-axle. So does a real car. A wheel-and-axle is a simple machine. It is made up of a wheel and an axle. An axle is a rod on which a wheel turns. The wheel and axle are connected so that they turn together. The axle turns when you turn the car's steering wheel. The axle moves the front wheels of the car. You do not have to turn the car's wheels with your hands. The wheel-and-axle does the work for you!

A wheel-and-axle simple machine uses two parts to move an object.

A wheel-and-axle makes work easier. This simple machine uses a circular motion to force an object to move.

How does a pulley work?

Have you ever seen a person raise a flag on Flag Day? The person used a pulley to do it. A pulley is a wheel with a rope, cord, or chain around it. One end of the rope hangs on each side of the pulley. To raise a flag you pull down on the rope on one side. The pull changes the direction of a force. On the other side of the pulley, the rope raises the flag. You do not have to climb to the top of the pole to raise the flag!

What are other simple machines?

A ramp is an inclined plane.

This chair is too heavy to lift into a truck. You can use an inclined plane to help you! An inclined plane is another simple machine. It is a flat board that is slanted. One end is higher than the other. It raises an object by moving it up a slope.

This inclined plane is attached to the back of the truck. The chair can be pushed up the inclined plane. Or, it can be pulled. It is easier to move an object up an inclined plane than it is to lift the object.

It's cold outside. Let's chop some wood to make a fire in the fireplace. An adult will use an ax as a wedge. A wedge is two inclined planes placed back to back. One edge is sharp and pointed. The other is wide and flat. A wedge is a tool that forces something apart. The pointed edge will split one thing into two pieces.

The blade of an ax splits the wood into two pieces.

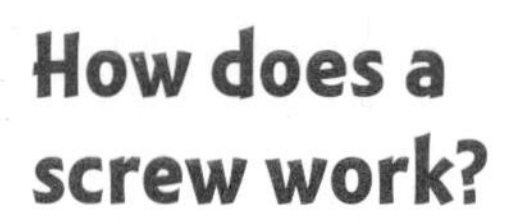

How does a screw work?

A screw is a simple machine. It uses circular motion to do work.

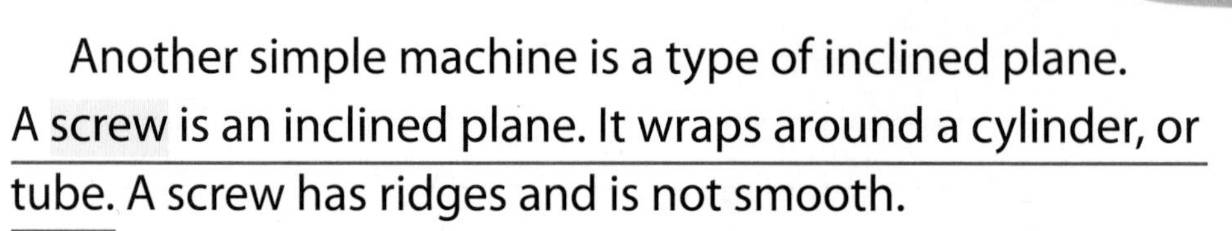

Another simple machine is a type of inclined plane. A screw is an inclined plane. It wraps around a cylinder, or tube. A screw has ridges and is not smooth.

Some screws are used to lower and raise things. A jar uses a screw to hold the lid on top. When you turn the lid, the screw raises or lowers the lid. A screw can also hold objects together. For example, you can use a screw to attach one piece of wood to another piece of wood.

What happens when we combine simple machines?

A compound machine is a machine that is made up of two or more simple machines. A compound machine can do more difficult jobs than a simple machine can do.

A hand-held can opener is a compound machine. It is three simple machines together. First, you use a lever to connect two arms onto the can. Next, you turn the handle to rotate the can. The handle works as a wheel-and-axle. Finally, a wedge, or circular wheel, cuts through the metal.

A lever, wheel-and-axle, and wedge work together in this compound machine. They help to open the can.

How do machines help us do work?

Machines make our lives much easier. They help us to do our work. Machines make difficult tasks easier.

Look at the picture of simple and compound machines. Workers use many machines to get their job done. The store sells other kinds of machines, too. They help people do work at home.

Think about the six kinds of simple machines you learned about: *lever, pulley, wheel-and-axle, inclined plane, wedge,* and *screw.* Look at the pictures. Which machines are simple machines? These are made up of few or no moving parts. Which machines are compound machines, made up two or more simple machines? Think about how these tools make people's lives much easier! How do these tools make people's lives much easier?

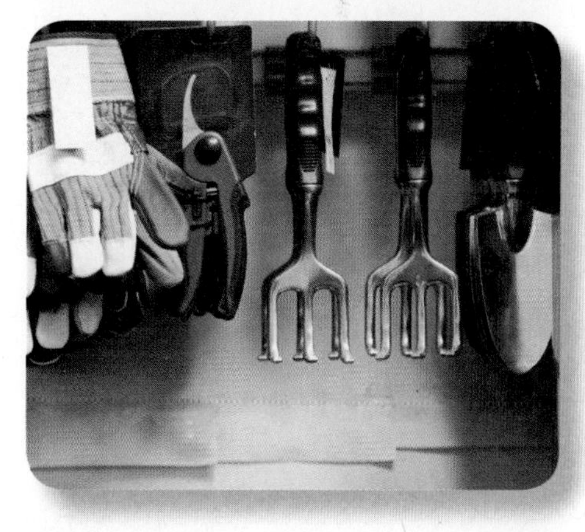

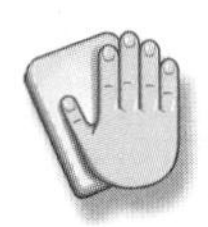

Conduct an Experiment

Work with a partner. Gather different kinds of tools, such as a hammer, shovel, pencil sharpener, skateboard, and paper cutter. With the help of an adult, show how to use each one. Put on things to keep you safe, such as goggles, gloves, or a helmet. Write the name of each machine in a notebook. Tell how it works.

Research and Report

Work with a partner. Learn more about the jobs scientists do. Use the Internet or other reference materials. Ask yourself questions: *What different tools do scientists use in experiments? How do these tools help scientists do their work?* Write a paragraph about what you learned. Draw pictures to show what scientists do. Share your report with the class.

Glossary

compound machine [KOM•pound muh•SHEEN] A machine that is made up of two or more simple machines. *A pencil sharpener is a compound machine because it is made up of a wedge and a wheel-and-axle.*

force [FOHRS] A push or a pull. *It takes a lot of force to push a table.*

fulcrum [FUHL•kruhm] The balance point of a lever that supports the arm but does not move. *A fulcrum is located at the center of a seesaw.*

gravity [GRAV•i•tee] A force that pulls two objects toward each other. *When I dropped the cup of juice, gravity caused it to fall to the ground.*

inclined plane [in•KLYND PLAYN] A simple machine that is a slanted surface. *The handicapped ramp at school is an example of an inclined plane.*

lever [LEV•er] A simple machine made up of a bar that pivots, or turns, on a fixed point. *I will use a lever to lift the lid off of this can.*

pulley [PUHL•ee] A simple machine made of a wheel with a rope, cord, or chain around it. *He will use a pulley to lift the bucket of water out of the well.*

screw [SKROO] A simple machine made of a post with an inclined plane wrapped around it. *She uses a screwdriver and screws to attach shelves to the bookcase.*

simple machine [SIM•puhl muh•SHEEN] A machine with few or no moving parts that you apply just one force to. *A hammer is an example of a simple machine.*

wedge [WEJ] A simple machine composed of two inclined planes back to back. *An ax is a simple machine called a wedge.*

weight [WAYT] A measure of the force of gravity on an object. *You can use a spring scale at the grocery store to measure the weight of fruits and vegetables.*

wheel-and-axle [WEEL AND AK•suhl] A simple machine made of a wheel and an axle that turn together. *A wheel-and-axle is used in a car to move the front wheels.*

work [WERK] The use of a force to move an object over a distance. *An example of work is pulling a wagon to carry toys.*